The Diving Beetle

This book has been reviewed
for accuracy by
Walter L. Gojmerac
Professor of Entomology
University of Wisconsin—Madison.

Library of Congress Cataloging in Publication Data

Oda, Hidetomo.
The diving beetle.

(Nature close-ups)
Translation of: Gengorō / text by Hidetomo Oda, photographs by Hidekazu Kubo.
Summary: Describes in text and photographs the life cycle, behavior, and natural habitat of the diving beetle.
1. Dytiscidae—Juvenile literature. [1. Water beetles. 2. Beetles] I. Kubo, Hidekazu, ill. II. Title. III. Series.
QL596.D903313 1986 595.76'2 85-28300

ISBN 0-8172-2533-1 (lib. bdg.)
ISBN 0-8172-2558-7 (softcover)

This edition first published in 1986 by Raintree Publishers Inc.

1 2 3 4 5 6 7 8 9 0 90 89 88 87 86

The Diving Beetle

Raintree Publishers
Milwaukee

◀ Diving beetles eating a carp.

Both young and adult diving beetles eat small underwater animals such as tadpoles, snails, and shrimp.

▶ A pond where diving beetles live.

Diving beetles prefer small, shallow bodies of water with little or no current.

Beneath the still surface of small ponds, lakes, and marshes, there is a hidden world of water insects. Many are beetles of one sort or another—whirligig beetles, water scavengers, and diving beetles. There are about a quarter of a million different kinds, or species, of beetles throughout the world. Of these, four thousand are species of diving beetles.

Diving beetles are among the biggest of the water beetles. Some are almost three inches long. They are excellent swimmers and fierce underwater hunters. Most diving beetles are brown or black and have yellow markings.

▶ A male (left) and female diving beetle.

The male has suction disks at the end of his front legs which he uses during mating. The female has no disks. This species of diving beetle is greenish black, but appears green under water.

◀ **A diving beetle hiding among leaves.**

When it senses danger, an adult diving beetle hides among water plants or under dead leaves at the bottom of the pond.

▶ **Diving beetles eating (photos 1-3).**

Diving beetles use their sense of smell to find food. They are attracted to the odor of decaying flesh. Here, a number of diving beetles gather to eat a dead crayfish.

Almost all species of diving beetles are hunters, or predators. They feed on small fish, water insects, worms, tadpoles, and snails. The larvae, the developing diving beetles, usually eat live animals. But the adults are scavengers. That is, they are attracted to dead and decaying flesh. Because they eat every part of an animal's remains, diving beetles are known as the "cleaners" of the pond. When one beetle finds a food source, other beetles soon gather around to share in the feast.

◀ **A diving beetle's strong jaws.**

With its strong, sharp jaws, called mandibles, the diving beetle is able to tear apart the food it eats.

1

2

3

◀ **A male and female diving beetle.**

During mating, the male fixes himself on the female's back by using his suction disks.

▶ **The male's suction disks.**

The male's suction disks are covered with tiny hairs. The hairs help him to cling to the female during mating.

Adult diving beetles mate in the spring, soon after they have awakened from their winter's sleep, or hibernation. During the mating process, the male climbs onto the back of the female. He uses his suction disks to cling to her because she is smooth and slippery. Mating may take from several hours to a full day, depending on the species of beetle. During the process, the male gives the female white bags filled with sperm. The sperm fertilize eggs that are in the female's body.

▼ When the female is ready to mate, she stops swimming. The male climbs on her back and gives her white bags filled with sperm.

▼ After the sperm have entered the female's body, she releases the empty white bag.

▲ **A female biting a hole.**

Around mating time, the female begins to nibble on water plants. When she is ready to lay her eggs, she busily bites tiny holes in the plant stem to serve as nests.

▲ **A diving beetle laying an egg.**

The female pokes her ovipositor into the nest she has made and lays an egg.

Soon after mating, the female diving beetle is ready to begin laying eggs. She chooses a place where there will be enough food for the larvae to eat as they grow. Some diving beetles lay their eggs on the leaves of underwater plants. Others bite tiny holes in plant stems, and the holes serve as nests for the eggs.

A tube for laying eggs extends from the back part of the female's body, the abdomen. The female uses this ovipositor to lay her eggs, one by one. The number of eggs laid depends on the species of diving beetle.

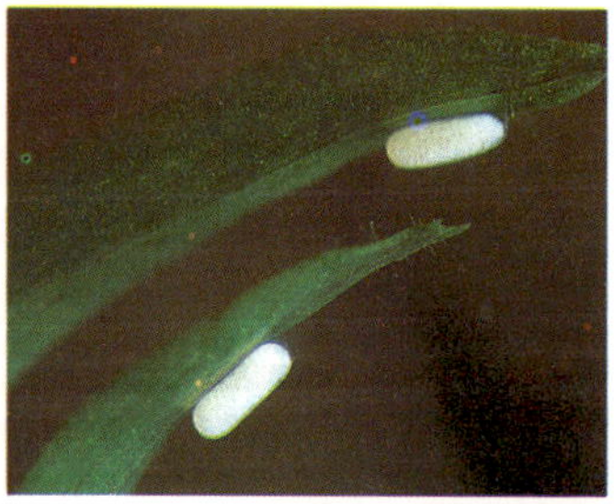

◀ **Diving beetle eggs.**

This species of diving beetle lays its long, banana-shaped eggs on underwater plant leaves.

▼ An egg laid inside a plant stem. The plant stem on the left shows the hole where a diving beetle egg has been laid. Inside the stem on the right, a week-old larva can be seen through the egg case.

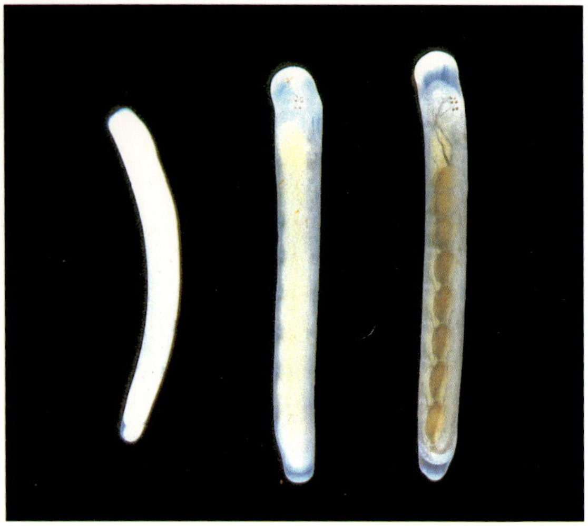

◀ **The egg develops.**

At first, only the long white egg is visible. Soon, the head and body of the larva can be seen as they begin to form inside the egg. In two to three weeks, the larva is ready to emerge.

▶ **A newly-emerged larva.**

The newly-emerged larva of this species is almost an inch long. It has a long, slender body with many joints, and it lives on the tops of waterweeds.

Within several weeks the larva emerges from, comes out of, the egg, and the diving beetle has entered the second stage of its life cycle. The larva is a strange-looking creature. It does not look like its parents at all.

Although their appearance varies greatly from species to species, all larvae have three distinct body parts. The head includes eyes and well-developed mouth parts. Three pairs of legs are attached to the larva's thorax, or mid-section. And the back part of the body is the long, segmented abdomen.

▼ **A diving beetle larva emerging (photos 1-6).**

The larva first sticks its head out of the hole made by the female diving beetle when she laid her eggs. Slowly, it emerges. Within a day, the larva's body will turn light brown.

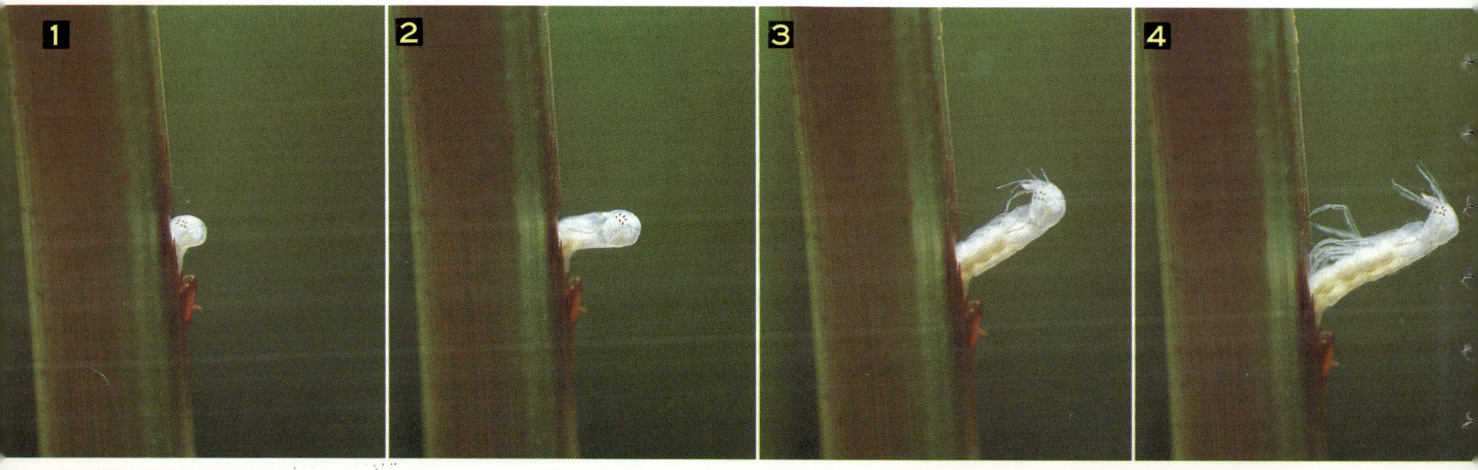

5

6

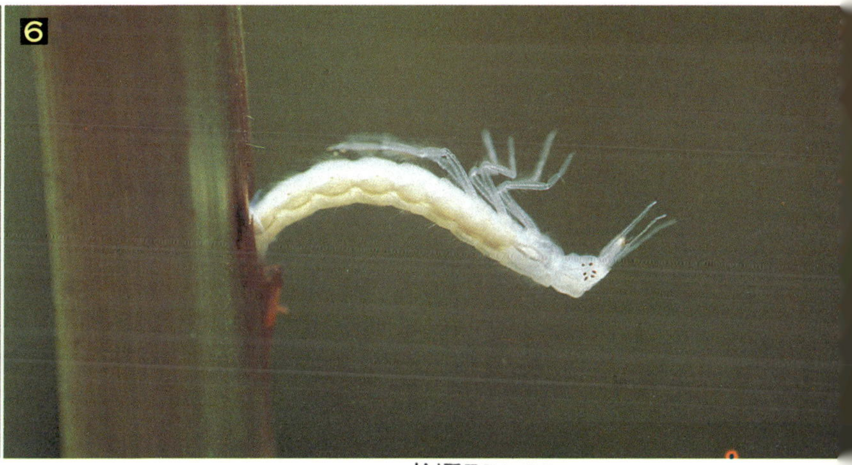

◀ **A larva seizes a striped-back midge.**

As the diving beetle larva sucks up the body fluids of this midge, the larva's body becomes tinged with red. Both larvae and adult diving beetles breathe oxygen from the air by sticking their abdomens above the water's surface.

▶ **The larva's sharp fangs.**

Its sharp fangs have earned the larva the nickname "water tiger." The black arrow in the photograph shows the larva's eyes. The eyes detect objects that are moving in the water.

Diving beetle larvae are ferocious predators. Moving easily on their long legs, they stalk their prey among the waterweeds. They hunt for worms, snails, fish, and other small water animals. The larvae look so fierce with their long, curved mandibles that they are often called "water tigers." When a larva catches an animal, it injects it with a substance that turns the victim's body parts to liquid. Then the larva sucks up its liquid meal.

▶ **A larva feasting on a minnow.**

After all the body fluids have been sucked from this minnow, only its skin and bones will remain.

◀ **A larva shedding its skin.**

Within a month, this species of diving beetle has outgrown its skin. The larva molts in shallow water where it can breathe easily.

▶ **A larva attacking a crayfish.**

As the larva grows larger, it becomes bolder. It sometimes attacks and eats prey much larger than itself.

Diving beetle larvae eat a great deal. Some mature larvae may devour thirty victims a day. Because the larvae eat so much, their bodies grow rapidly. But their skin does not grow. So the larvae must molt, or shed their skin, as their bodies get bigger. Some species of diving beetles molt three times, others a great many more. Each stage of molting is called an instar. Most diving beetle larvae are full grown and have molted for the last time within five to six weeks.

▼ **A larva attacking a small fish (photos 1-3).**

This larva stalks among the waterweeds, looking for prey. When a victim comes near, the larva reaches out with its strong jaws and seizes it.

◀ **A larva leaving the pond.**

This larva has grown to almost three inches by the time it is ready to leave the pond and become a pupa.

▶ **A larva in its pupal chamber.**

The larva uses its head and mandibles to dig up the wet soil. It prepares a chamber where it can rest during the pupal stage of its development.

When the larva has reached its full growth, it is ready to enter the next stage in its life cycle—as a pupa. During the pupal stage, the larva becomes an adult. In some species, the larva digs into the bottom of the pond to pupate. In others, the larva leaves the pond and comes ashore to burrow its hole. Hooking its sharp mandibles into the ground, it drags itself up the bank of the pond. Then it digs a hole in the wet soil and prepares a pupal chamber where it can rest. While the larva rests, mysterious changes take place.

▶ **A larva digging its pupal chamber.**

In its last days as a larva, the diving beetle spends its time in the shallows of the pond before it comes ashore to begin digging its chamber.

▲ **A pupa emerging (photos 1-3).** Five days after its pupal chamber is completed, this larva begins to pupate, or leave its skin. First, the back of its skin splits open. Finally, a fat white pupa emerges from inside.

A few days after the diving beetle larva has entered its pupal chamber, it undergoes a radical change. The larval skin splits down the middle of its back, and a plump white body with large black eyes and long fat legs comes out. This pale, mummy-like creature is the pupa. Although the pupa appears to be resting, changes are taking place inside its body. In a few species of diving beetles, the larva spins a cocoon to protect itself during this dormant period.

◀ **A larva that has failed to pupate.**

The pupal stage is a dangerous time for the diving beetle. A severe change in temperature or humidity could kill it. Sometimes, the larva cannot shed its skin properly. This larva was not able to shed the skin around its head. It cannot move, and it will soon die.

▼ **A newly emerged pupa.**

This white pupa has completely shed its old larval skin. Inside the new pupal skin, the adult diving beetle's body has now begun to form.

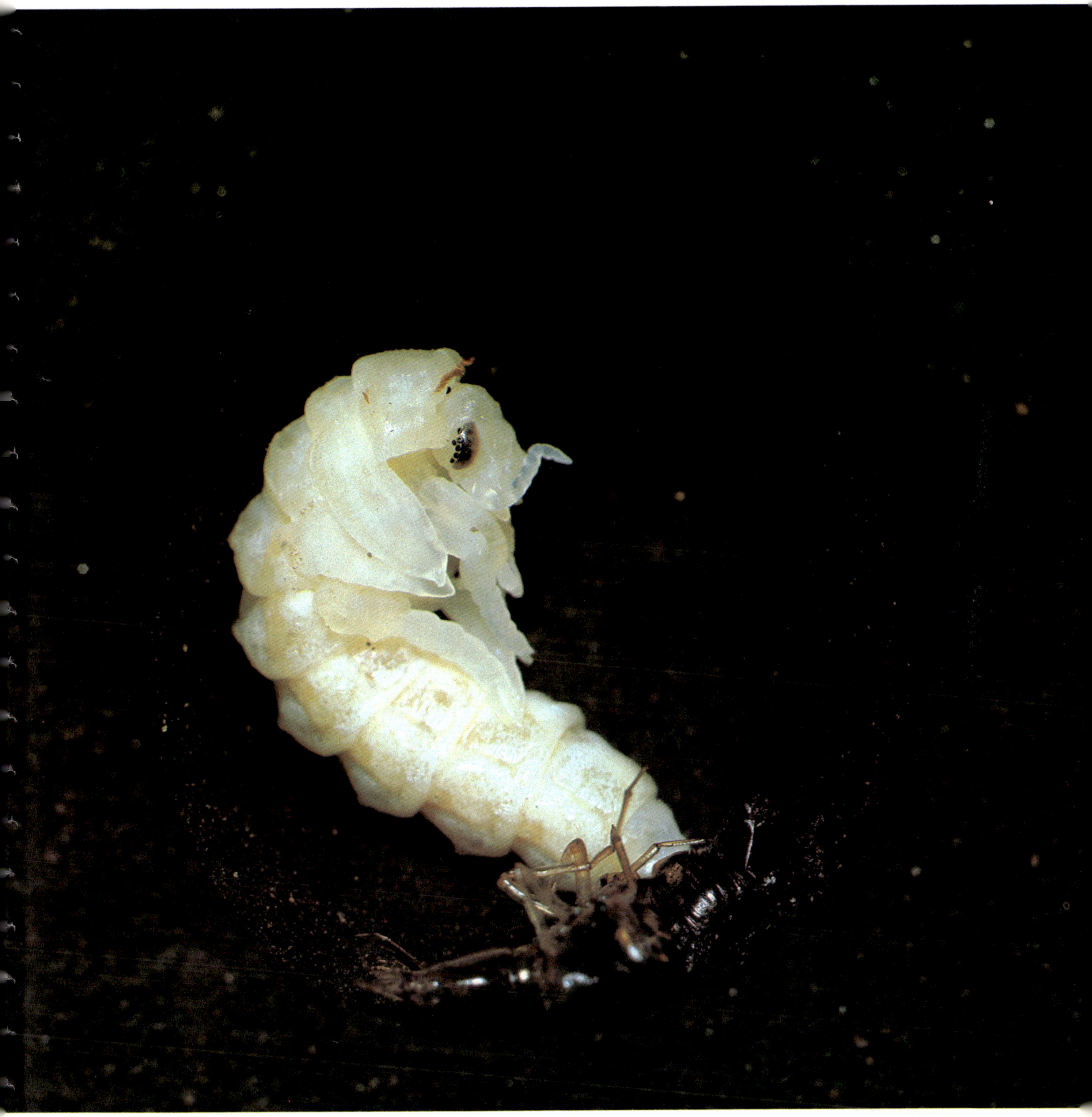

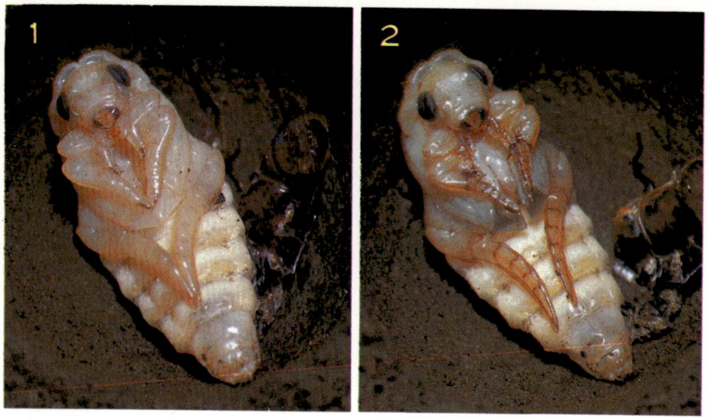

◀ **The adult beetle begins to form (photos 1-2).**

Inside the resting pupa, the legs of the adult diving beetle begin to form. Later, the white skin of the pupa darkens.

▶ **An adult unfolding its wings.**

When it has completely shed its pupal skin, the adult diving beetle unfolds its wings and waits for them to expand.

Inside the pupa, the body of the adult diving beetle begins to form. Soon the legs and the abdomen become visible through the white pupal skin. In about ten days, the pupa is ready to molt. The pupal skin splits open and the adult diving beetle begins to emerge. Slowly, it pulls its front wings and head from the old skin. Then it pulls out its legs and abdomen. The beetle stretches out its wrinkled wings and waits for them to become full size. The adult diving beetle is colorless when it first emerges, but its skin will soon darken.

▼ **An adult diving beetle emerging (photos 1-6).**

The pupal skin splits open and a pure white adult slowly emerges and expands its wings.

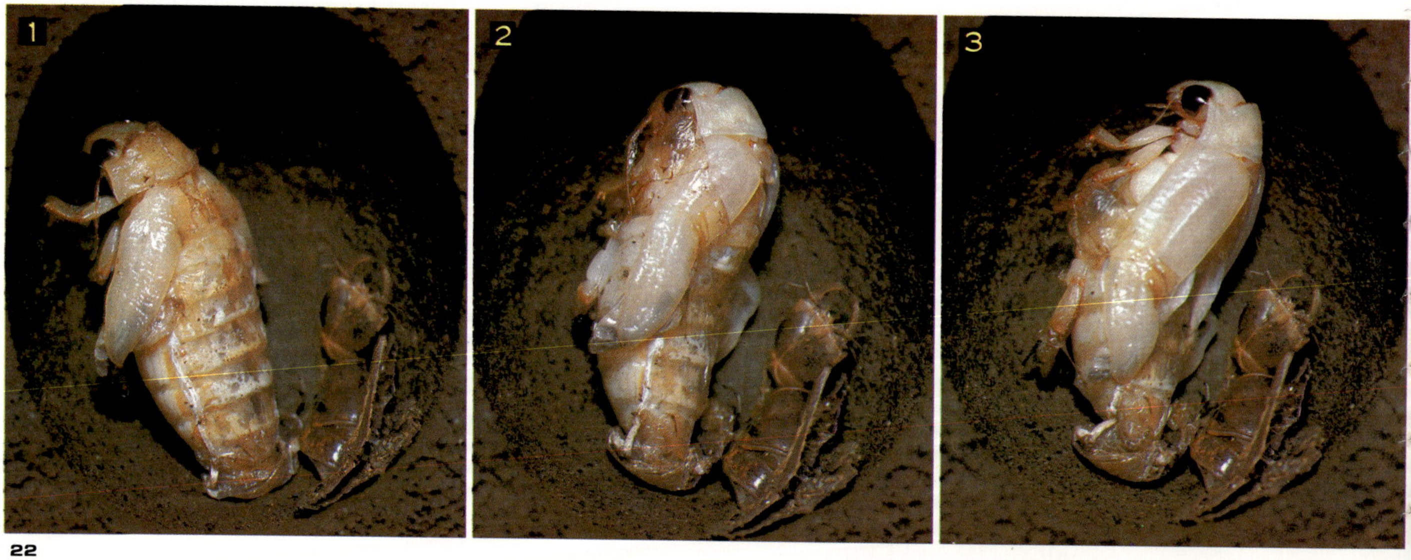

4

5

6

◀ **An adult diving beetle returning to the pond.**

When it reaches the pond, this diving beetle does not dive in immediately. Instead, it floats on the surface, perhaps getting used to the water.

▶ **Adult diving beetles swimming.**

This is a view of the underside of two diving beetles as they swim among the waterweeds.

Once the diving beetle becomes a winged adult, it has entered the final stage in its life cycle. It is now full grown and will not molt again. But the diving beetle must wait, perhaps for several days, before it leaves its underground nest. During that time, its front pair of wings hardens. They form the elytra, a wing case that protects the fragile, transparent hind wings. As the front wings harden, the beetle's body darkens in color. After it leaves the pupal chamber, the diving beetle instinctively returns to its life in the water.

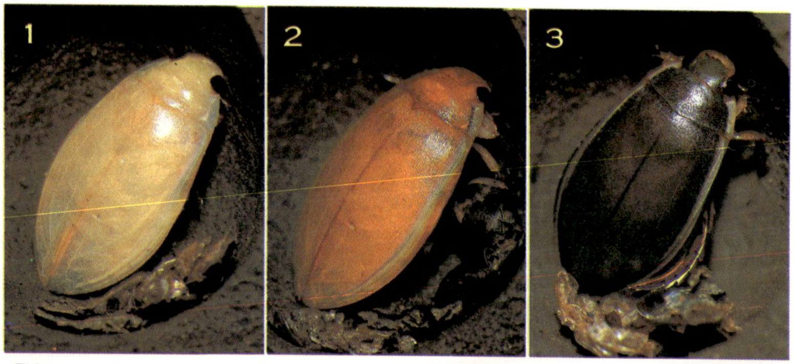

◀ **The beetle's body darkens (photos 1-3).**

Within twenty-four hours, this species of diving beetle changes from white to orange to brown to greenish black. A few days later the beetle's body hardens, and it leaves its underground nest.

◀ **A diving beetle carrying a crayfish.**

▶ **A diving beetle (left) and a water scavenger (right).**

The diving beetle moves its right and left legs at the same time when it swims. The water scavenger moves it legs separately and is not such a good swimmer.

The adult diving beetle is an excellent swimmer. In fact, it is the best swimmer in the water beetle family. Its flat, dish-shaped body helps it move easily through the water. Its powerful oar-like hind legs are covered with tiny hairs, which propel it quickly through the water. Unlike some beetles, the diving beetle moves its right and left legs at the same time as it paddles through the water. This rhythm helps it to stay on course and to move quickly. In fact, the diving beetle swims so well that it can carry large prey with it as it swims.

▶ **The hind legs of two different beetles.**

The diving beetle has wide flat legs, which look like oars, and are covered with fine hairs (left). The water scavenger's legs are slender and more suited to walking than swimming (right).

◀ **A diving beetle breathing.**

A diving beetle takes air in at the tip of its abdomen. It stores the air under its wings, which allows it to stay underwater for a long time.

▶ **Smaller diving beetles carrying air bubbles.**

Smaller beetles carry permanent air bubbles which enable them to stay underwater for hours at a time. When the oxygen from the air is used up, the bubble takes in oxygen from the water and passes out carbon dioxide.

Although diving beetles spend their lives underwater, they must come to the surface to breathe. They float head down with just the tips of their abdomens sticking above water to breathe in oxygen from the air. Diving beetles can stay underwater a long time because they store air and take it with them. Large beetles store air in a space between their wings and abdomen. Smaller beetles carry permanent air bubbles at the tips of their abdomens.

▼ Tubes for breathing.

The diving beetle has two tubes at the end of its abdomen. It extends them above the water in order to breathe.

▼ A spiracle.

Stored air is taken into the beetle's body through tiny openings in its abdomen, called spiracles. The arrow points to a spiracle which is located just behind the wings.

◀ **A diving beetle in flight.**

The hind wings are used mostly for flying. The front wing covers are held out, motionless, on either side, like the wings of an airplane. They give the beetle "lift."

▶ **A pond where beetles are hibernating (upper) and diving beetles hibernating (lower).**

Diving beetles hibernate in dead leaves and dried grasses at the bottom of ponds. They live on food that they store up from the previous summer.

In addition to being good swimmers, diving beetles can also fly. The hardened front wings, the elytra, are raised in flight but remain still. They help to give the beetle "lift." It is the hind wings which beat up and down, moving the beetle forward.

At night diving beetles fly from pond to pond in search of food. And in autumn, they fly about looking for a place to spend the winter. During the cold winter, most adult diving beetles hibernate at the bottom of small lakes and ponds. In spring they awaken and look for a mate.

◀ **A diving beetle sunbathing.**

Diving beetles come out of the water to sunbathe. The sunshine prevents mold and algae from growing on their bodies, and it helps keep them healthy. Some species produce a chemical that cleans surface bacteria and slime from their bodies.

GLOSSARY

abdomen—the back, or rear section, of an insect's body. (pp. 10, 12, 28)

fertilized—when a sperm and an egg unite, making it possible for a new organism to form. (p. 9)

instinct—behavior with which an animal is born, rather than behavior which is learned. (p. 24)

mandibles—jaws that are used for biting and chewing. (pp. 6, 15, 19)

ovipositor—an egg-laying tube that extends from the tip of an insect's abdomen. (p. 10)

predator—an animal that hunts or kills other animals for food. (pp. 6, 15)

prey—animals that are killed by predators. (pp. 15, 16, 27)

scavenger—an animal that feeds on dead or decaying animal matter. (p. 6)

species—a group of animals which scientists have identified as having common traits. (pp. 5, 6, 12)

sperm—a mature male germ cell. (p. 9)

suction disks—special disks on the male diving beetle's front legs with which he holds onto the female during mating. (pp. 5, 9)

thorax—an insect's mid-section, to which legs and sometimes wings are attached. (p. 12)